AF153853

H.C. Eastman

Eastman's Treatise on Counterfeit, Altered and Spurious Bank Notes

Anatiposi

H.C. Eastman

Eastman's Treatise on Counterfeit, Altered and Spurious Bank Notes

Reprint of the original.

1st Edition 2023 | ISBN: 978-3-38230-790-5

Anatiposi Verlag is an imprint of Outlook Verlagsgesellschaft mbH.

Verlag (Publisher): Outlook Verlag GmbH, Zeilweg 44, 60439 Frankfurt, Deutschland
Vertretungsberechtigt (Authorized to represent): E. Roepke, Zeilweg 44, 60439 Frankfurt, Deutschland
Druck (Print): Books on Demand GmbH, In de Tarpen 42, 22848 Norderstedt, Deutschland

MONEY

EASTMAN'S

TREATISE ON COUNTERFEIT, ALTERED AND SPURIOUS

BANK NOTES,

WITH UNERRING RULES FOR THE DETECTION OF
FRAUDS IN THE SAME,

TOGETHER WITH

A HISTORY OF ANCIENT MONEY, CONTINENTAL CURRENCY, BANKS,
BANKING, BANK OF ENGLAND, AND OTHER VALUABLE
INFORMATION AS TO

MONEY,

WITH HINTS TO BUSINESS SUCCESS.

BY H. G. EASTMAN,

AUTHOR OF EASTMAN'S COMPLETE ACCOUNT BOOK AND TIME TABLE, AND
PRESIDENT OF EASTMAN'S COMMERCIAL COLLEGE,
ST. LOUIS, MO., AND OSWEGO, N. Y.

THIRD EDITION—ENLARGED.

PRINTED BY M. NIEDNER, NO. 43 PINE STREET.

1859.

CONTENTS.

4

DEPARTMENT
FOR DETECTING
COUNTERFEIT, ALTERED
AND
SPURIOUS
BANK NOTES, CHECKS,
Drafts, &c.,
IN
EASTMAN'S COMMERCIAL COLLEGE.

TERMS:

(Students and others receiving instruction in this branch, at the College, are exercised with a great variety of both Genuine and Counterfeit Plates, making it the most ready and reliable means extant, and taught in no other Institution in the Union, with equal success (see Eastman's Money Treatise). All Students who enter for the *" Full Commercial Course"* in this Institution, receive full and complete instruction in this branch, free of charge).

Persons from the city or abroad, who desire instruction, will apply at the College, on Fourth Street, corner of Vine and St. Charles, from 9 to 12, A. M.

For a full Course of Instruction, developing the entire principle upon which all Genuine Bank Notes are constructed, with illustrations of Counterfeit and Genuine Work and Certificate, ... $5 00

All persons receiving instruction will be furnished with a copy of *" Eastman's Treatise on Bank Notes, Money, etc., etc."*

MONEY.

"Put money in thy purse," was the crafty advice of Iago, and from time past memory the world has adopted and acted on this happy suggestion. Not that in the "guinea's stamp," in itself considered, there is hidden any such talismanic virtue, but simply because society has adopted the piece of stamped metal as its most convenient medium for facilitating exchanges. The oxen with which Diomede paid for his armor, the iron currency of Sparta, the Belt of Wampum of the North American Indian, answered the same purpose as do now the Bank Bill or the Gold Eagle.

As individual wants become more varied and numerous, the necessity for a convenient circulating medium, not as property, but as the *representative* of property, becomes correspondingly great; and as the result of this advanced civilization, we see the whole machinery of Government, every department of Society, working by means of these forces so insignificant in themselves—Guineas, Eagles, Dollars. These constitute in themselves the Trinity in which all believe. None are so incredulous as to doubt the mission of money; none repudiate the "Almighty Dollar."

Nor can it be regarded as extravagant to say that the whole fabric of society and of national and individual opulence, resting as it does to so great an extent on this metallic and paper basis, will stand securely only so long as confidence exists in the purity and substantiality of that basis.

The objections to a purely "hard money" or metallic circulating medium, which so readily suggest themselves to every business man, have given increased importance to Banks and Bank Bills, and accordingly by an almost universal custom, Bank Bills are received and treated as money, in the business of life, in the making of exchanges, and in all the details of a business community.

The commanding importance of moneyed institutions in their relations to modern society justify the observation of a distinguished American critic, that as " Temples were the Banks of Greece, Banks are the Temples of America.

The chief objection which is made or can be made to a paper currency, is the facility with which in the present state of engraving, the issues of Banks may be counterfeited or altered. The extent to which " Bills" are received, and the frequency of counterfeited or altered bills justify, as it seems, the publication of the system of rules given in the following pages for the detection of frauds in these particulars.

ANCIENT MONEY.

Before the invasion of Julius Cæsar the natives of England had tin plates, iron plates, and rings, which were received as money. On the authority of Seneca a curious account is given, where leather appropriately stamped to give it a certain legal character, was the only current money. At a comparatively recent date in the annals of Europe, Frederick the Second, at the siege of Milan, actually paid his troops in leather money. Nearly the same circumstance occurred in England during the great Wars of the Barons. The crown of Queen Philippa, which had been pawned at Cologne for £2,500, was redeemed by sending over three hundred and thirty-four and a half sacks of wool. In the course of 1250, King John, for the ransom of his royal person, promised to pay Edward III. of England, three millions of gold crowns. In order to fulfil the obligation, he was reduced to the mortifying necessity of paying the expenses of the palace in leather money, in the centre of each piece being a bright point of silver. In that reign is found the origin of the travestied honor of boyhood called—conferring a leather medal. The imposing ceremonies accompanying a presentation gave full force, dignity and value to a leather jewel, which noblemen were probably proud and grateful to receive at the hands of Majesty.

As late as 1574 there was an immense issue of money in Holland stamped on small sheets of pasteboard. But further back in the vista of years, Numa Pompilius, the Second King of Rome, who reigned six hundred and twenty-two years before the Christian Era, made money out of wood as well as leather. Both gold and silver appear to have been in extensive circulation in Egypt soon after their potency was understood in Asia. Thence they were introduced into Carthage and Greece, and finally travelling farther and farther in a Westerly direction, Rome discovered the importance of legalizing their circulation as money.

Weight having always been of the first importance in early times, the shape of money appears to have been a matter of perfect indifference for a series of years. When the small pieces or portions of metal received as precious, were extensively circulated, it is quite probable that each person shaped them to suit his own convenience as is practised to some extent at this time in remote portions of the East Indies. There the payer cuts off parts with shears till he obtains by exact weight the stipulated price. It was thus that men traveled with the evidence of their possessions in a sack. But great inconvenience must have resulted from this often tedious process, and as nations advanced in civilization and the economic arts, a certain mark or impression on pieces of a certain size caused them to be acknowledged each as the representative of a certain sum of money. This facilitated negotiations, and afterwards led to further improvements, both in the shape, weight and beauty of the external devices. The custom which has prevailed for a long series of years in all the nations of Europe, of stamping the medallion likeness of the reigning Sovereign on the coin newly issued, enables us to read the history of their successive dynasties in the faces on the National Currency. So that the "stamped metal" answers a two-fold purpose. The "guinea's stamp" becomes a history in itself, which as Hood sings—

——"Even its minted coins express
Now stamped with the image of good Queen Bess,
And now of a bloody Mary."

CONTINENTAL CURRENCY.

Money, as well as patriotism, is needed for the defence of any country. In the contest which established American Independence patriotism was not lacking, but the money in many instances was lamentably deficient. The Congress of the United States experienced great difficulty in providing the requisite means for carrying on hostilities, and to supply this want, May 10, 1775, soon after the battle of Lexington, Congress made preparations to issue three millions of Continental Paper—two millions of which was put in circulation on June 22nd following. When first issued, this money was everywhere at par, and proved of great utility to the army and country generally. In 1790, when nearly three millions had been issued, it began to depreciate. Rumors gained circulation that Congress would not redeem these bills, which although promptly denied, caused great loss to holders. Forty dollars of this money would bring but *one* of gold or silver, and the evil was aggravated by inadequate remedies.

"The paper," says Lossing, "at its nominal value, was made a legal tender for all debts ; and, by this measure, which Washington deeply deplored, many creditors, both public and private, were defrauded, but no permanent relief could be afforded, for confidence was destroyed. As the articles furnished the army, like all others, rose to an enormous nominal value, Congress, very injudiciously, fixed a maximum price, above which the articles to be purchased, should not be received. The consequence was, that at this stipulated rate, none could be got, and the army would assuredly have perished had not this absurd regulation been speedily rescinded."

These issues continued to depreciate until eventually they became entirely valueless, and many of the officers and soldiers of the army were ruined, and themselves and their families were reduced to beggary.

BANKS.

The word Bank is derived from the Italian word " *Banco*," meaning a bench. The Jews, who were the first to follow the business of lending money, were accustomed to assemble in the market places in Italian towns, seated on benches, there to transact their business. The term " bankrupt" was first applied to those whose seats or benches were broken up or removed when they failed in business. Banks are of three kinds, Banks of Deposit, Banks of Discount, and Banks of Circulation. The earliest establishment of the latter kind, in Europe, was founded near the close of the 12th century, and was called the Bank of Venice. This was the earliest Bank of Circulation on the Continent. As a bank of deposit, however, it had had an existence for ten years previous to this time.

A plan of a National Bank was first proposed in this country by Robert Morris, of Pennsylvania, the distinguished financier and statesman, and was submitted to Congress on May 17, 1781, and passed that body on the 26th of the same month. The Bank commenced operation with a capital of four hundred thousand dollars, in January following. In 1790 Alexander Hamilton, then Secretary of the Treasury, urged upon Congress the importance of establishing a United States Bank. Though violently opposed, this measure was adopted in the following year, as the only feasible mode of restoring public credit and of discharging the many foreign and domestic debts, incurred by Congress, as well as the several States, in carrying on the War of the Revolution. The bank commenced operations with a capital of ten millions of dollars, divided into twenty-five thousand shares. The dividends of the bank did not, at any time during its existence of twenty years exceed 10 per cent. per annum. The application made in 1808 for a renewal of the charter was opposed, as had been the first attempts at incorporation. The application was unsuccessful, and, in 1811, the bank was obliged to wind up its affairs.

On April 3rd, 1816, a bill for a second Bank of the United States passed both Houses, was signed by the President, and became a law; the charter extended to March 3rd, 1836. The bank went into operation January 7, 1817. On July 10th, 1832, the President refused to sign a bill re-chartering the bank, and returned it with a message stating his objections. At the expiration of the Charter granted by the United States March 1836, it was immediately rechartered by the State of Pennsylvania. On October 9th, 1839, it suspended specie payment for a second time, and on February 4th following suspended entirely, leaving nothing to its stockholders, its entire capital having been sunk, spreading disaster throughout the country.

In 1784, the first bank, other than those already mentioned, which went into operation in any of the States, was established in the city of Boston. The Manhattan Bank was next established in New York in 1799, and is now in operation, this was the commencement of Banking in that State. From that time banks have increased until they are scattered over all parts of the Union, and now number, inclusive of branches, not far from 1500, with an aggregate capital of $1,055,291,573.

ORIGIN OF THE BANK OF ENGLAND.

As late as the Restoration, every merchant of "Merrie England" kept a strong box in his own house. When an acceptance was presented to him, he counted out the crowns or Caroluses. Those were the halcyon days of thieves, when a burglar would, not unfrequently. be able, after a single night's work, to retire with a fortune ; when highway robbery was a lucrative profession, and its adepts were styled " gentlemen of the road."

By the end of Charles First's reign it was discovered that it was safer and more convenient to have agents to keep the cash of commercial houses. This new branch of business fell naturally into the hands of goldsmiths, who were accustomed to traffic largely in the precious metals, and who had vaults where masses of bullion could be kept secure from fire and robbers. It was at the shops of the goldsmiths of Lombard street, that all the payments in coin were made. Other traders gave and received nothing but paper.

But the same reasons which led the community to gather their cash into fifty vaults, instead of leaving it scattered among a thousand, soon led them to see that it would be still better to keep it in one, instead of fifty. In William the Third's time the matter was freely discussed, and in 1694 it took the definite shape of a plan for a National Bank. The idea first originated with Mr. William Patterson, a merchant of London. It was brought to the attention of the King, submitted to the Privy Council, and when the details were completed, it was laid before Parliament. The bill became a law on April 25, 1694, and the bank was open for business on January 1st, 1695. It gained popular favor, less by argument, than by its manifest convenience and utility. It lived, grew and prospered, and England has lived and grown and prospered with it. The stability of the Bank of England is almost equal to that of the British Government. All that it has advanced to the Government must be lost before the creditors can sustain any considerable loss.

A VISIT TO THE BANK OF ENGLAND.

The traveller who neglects to call and see " The Old Lady of Threadneedle street," as the Bank of England is familiarly called, denies himself a visit to the greatest of England's "lions."

As you approach the remarkable building in which the immense business of the Bank is carried on you observe an edifice of no particular architectural beauty ; possessing no imposing or marked grandeur calculated to awe the observer, and yet as you stand before an Institution that exerts more moral and political power than any Sovereign in Europe, you feel yourself in the presence of more than regal majesty. You have a burning curiosity to penetrate into the interior of this mighty and mysterious building, looming up before you, and to do so you must first obtain an order from the Governor of the Bank. On presenting your card of admission you are admitted into a private room where a messenger is ready to conduct you through the different apartments, which cover an area of eight acres of ground. There are no windows on the sides of the building, or towards the streets, each apartment being lighted from the roof of the enclosed areas.

The first apartment we enter is the vault where the Directors and Cashier are counting bags of gold which men are pitching down to them from a *store room* above. Each bag contains a thousand pounds sterling, fresh from the mint, never having been opened. We next enter a room where the notes of the Bank, received the day before, are being examined. Each note is carefully compared with the entries in the books, checked, and then placed in boxes to be stored away. It will be remembered that the Bank of England never issues the same note a second time, and to meet this immense demand for notes so constantly used, (and when returned are destroyed,) the Bank has its own paper makers, its own printers, its own engravers, all at work under the same roof. Even the machinery by which its work is done is made in the same building. It receives in the ordinary course of business upwards of *eight hundred thousand pounds* or nearly *four millions of dollars daily* in notes. These are put up in parcels according to their denominations, then securely boxed up, labeled with their denomination and date of reception, and placed in the vault to remain for ten years. If in the course of these ten years any dispute in business or litigation arises concerning the payment of any note, the bank is able to produce the identical bill. At the expiration of the ten years the notes are taken out and ground up in the mill to be made into notes again. Into the room, where the bank note paper is manufactured, we are next led. The process of manufacture is carefully conducted. The paper is manufactured with the greatest care from the finest of linen rags. It passes off from the machines in narrow sheets, stamped on both sides with eccentric ruled or engraved plates in lines, with letters expressing the denomination of the bills. The most beautiful, and yet complicated, operation in the whole bank, is a register extending from the printing machinery in this room to the general banking office in another part of the building. This register marks every sheet of paper that is struck off from the press, and at the same time records it in the banking office, so that not a note can be manufactured by the persons employed that is not recorded in this office. A similar register or shaft passes through all parts of this immense building, touching at every apartment and terminating in the general banking office. To this shaft is also attached sixteen clocks, in different parts of the establishment, and the whole is regulated with such a nicety of precision, that they never vary a second of time, and the whole sixteen strike the alarm the same moment.

In another room we find the weighers assorting the gold to detect the light coins. The machine is simple and resembles the letter weigher in common use. The coins are placed so as to slide one by one upon the spring scale, and if the piece of gold is of the standard weight the scale rises to a certain height and the piece slides off, if less than the standard weight, it rises a little higher and the coin slides off on the other side. We may watch the operation of this machine for many minutes, without discovering a coin under weight, and if we venture to ask what is the average number of light coins to a hundred or thousand of standard weight, we are politely informed by the messenger that that is a question which the weigher is not allowed to answer, and that he is not allowed to know the number himself. We next enter the engravers room, where are found more persons employed than in any other apartment. Some two thousand workmen altogether are employed in the building. The system of engraving seemed to be almost perfect, the various parts of a note being engraved by different artists, each one making a speciality of his part, and therefore excelling in execution of his particular task. The last room entered is that in which the notes are deposited which are ready for use. Here some twenty persons are engaged arranging and cording the stacks of money that surround us on every side, and here in the presence of thirty million pounds sterling or one hundred and fifty millions of dollars, we may perhaps form some idea of the magnitude of the business done, and the power this mass of money exerts over the entire civilized world.

If England is, as some one has sarcastically said " but a nation of shop keepers," its capacious " till," which we have thus been examining, affords the surest guaranty of their substantial wealth and commanding business importance.

GOLD IN CIRCULATION.

As near as can be estimated the amount of gold in circulation is not far from $240,000,000, which is subject to a wear or waste of about 4 per cent. per annum.

The consumption of gold in different arts and in manufactures is very large, and is variously computed at from thirty to forty millions of dollars a year. We have the authority of a London journal for the statement that in Birmingham there is a weekly consumption of gold, for chains alone, amounting to one thousand ounces. The weekly consumption of gold leaf in London is four hundred ounces, and one of the Potteries in Staffordshire consumes $3,500 worth of gold annually in gilding porcelain. The whole consumption for gilding porcelain in England is estimated at about five hundred ounces annually. This estimate, of course, has reference only to certain portions of England. If we add to this the immense sums annually expended for gold in manu- factories on the Continent and in America, our statement above will be found to be rather below than above the actual quantity.

THE DOLLAR MARK. ($.)

Much controversy has arisen as to the origin and meaning of the peculiar mark used to denote dollars. Some have attributed it to a corruption of the two letters U. S., used to represent Federal Cur- rency, which afterwards, in the hurry of writing, were run into one, the U. being first made and the S. put over it. Some writers say that it is derived from the contraction of the Spanish word *pesos*, "dollars;" others, from the Spanish *feutes*, "hard," to distinguish silver from paper money. The more probable expla- nation is, however, that it is a modification of the figure "8," having reference to eight reals, as the dollar was formerly called. The word dollar itself is regarded as derived from the German "Thaler."

WHAT CONSTITUTES A LEGAL TENDER.

———

This is regulated entirely by law. The Constitution of the United States vests in Congress the exclusive power " to coin money, regulate the value thereof, and of foreign coin." Nor can any State enact any law which shall make anything but gold and silver coin a tender in payment of debts. It is proper to add, however, in this connection, that bank notes are considered as a sufficient tender, unless objection is specifically made to them. The decisions of the Courts in the several States are tending strongly in favor of regarding bank notes, judicially as well as commercially, money.

Congress has fixed by law the respective sums for which coin issued by it from its mint shall be received as a legal tender, as also of the rates of foreign coins current in the United States.

The gold eagle is a legal tender for the payment of ten dollars. The half eagle for five dollars; and the quarter eagle for two and a half dollars. The double eagle is made a legal tender for twenty dollars. By the above is meant that gold coins are legal tender for the payment of all sums equal to or above their respective denomination.

The gold dollar is a legal tender for one dollar. The silver dollar, half-dollar, quarter-dollar, dime and half-dime are declared to be legal tender in payment of debts, for all sums not exceeding five dollars. The three cent piece is a legal tender in payment for all sums of thirty cents and under. Copper coins are not recognized as money, and are not good as a legal tender for any sum.

———

AMERICAN BANK NOTE COMPANY.

The following constitute, it is believed all of the firms now engaged in the business of *Bank Note Engraving and Printing*, in the United States, with the names of the places where their business is conducted. They have recently become associated under the name of the "American Bank Note Company," and have been duly incorporated. As such, their ability to execute whatever may be entrusted to them, both as to design and finish cannot be questioned:

Rawdon, Wright, Hatch & Edson, New York, Montreal, Cincinnati and New Orleans; and with Isaac Cary, The New England Bank Note Company, Boston; George Matthews, Montreal; Toppan, Carpenter & Co., New York, Philadelphia, Cincinnati and Boston; Danforth, Perkins & Co., (late Danforth, Wright & Co.,) New York, Philadelphia, Cincinnati and Boston; Bald, Cousland & Co., New York and Philadelphia; Jocelyn, Draper, Welsh & Co., New York; Draper, Welsh & Co., New York, Philadelphia and Boston; Wellstood, Hay & Whiting, New York and Chicago; John E. Gavitt, Albany.

BANK NOTES.

THEIR COUNTERFEITS AND MEANS OF PREVENTION.

COUNTERFEIT NOTES are those which are *intended* to be fac-similes of the genuine.

SPURIOUS NOTES are those which differ entirely from the genuine.

ALTERED NOTES are those whose title, locality, or denomination, has been extracted and some other one pasted or printed in its place. The term "raised note," is sometimes applied to those bills in which the *actual* denomination has been eaten or cut out, and in its place another and larger denomination put over or *raised* by a die ; sometimes it is done by hand.

The increase of Counterfeit, Altered and Spurious Bank Notes, during the last few years, and the immense losses sustained by the public in consequence of their *general* and constant circulation, demand that some measure of prevention should be adopted. The subject is daily acquiring a new interest. It was only during the last year that a bank in New York took six hundred dollars in counterfeit bills on its own institution, and in this city, [St. Louis,] quite recently, a Daguerreotypist, experimenting on the efficiency of Photography as a means of counterfeiting, presented a photographed check to a bank, which, on presentation to the cashier, was promptly paid.

The people of the United States lose in almost every form by paper money. The trade of the counterfeiter is now carried on to such an alarming extent, that the great number of counterfeits is regarded as the weightiest objection to a paper currency, and until the community becomes familiar with the characteristics of genuine bank notes, and the characteristics of a genuine engraving, they cannot escape heavy losses and imposition from counterfeits.

I propose in this work to familiarize the reader with the basis upon which all genuine bank notes are constructed, to give illustrations in counterfeit and genuine work, until becoming thoroughly familiar with the principal points of each ; he will obtain thereby an infallible key to the detection of all fraudulent issues.

BANK NOTE PAPER.

THE CHIEF SAFE GUARD AGAINST COUNTERFEITS, is in the manufacture of the paper on which the bills are intended to be printed.

A Chemist of New Haven has invented a yellowish or orange colored dye, with which the paper is stained, and which is said to be indelible and to prevent all attempts at change or eradication. Several of the New England Banks have since employed his process. The Art of Photography has so materially contributed to the trade of counterfeiters, that the Directors of the Bank of England, in order most effectually to put a stop to the possibility of fraud being perpetrated to so alarming an extent, by that agency, have entirely altered the color of the paper on which their notes are *printed*, as well as changed the color of the ink used in printing them, and substituted a widely different shade. From inquiries and experiments which have been made, it is ascertained that, if the notes be printed on yellow tinged paper, in blue ink, it is impossible, or *at least* extremely difficult, to transfer fac-similes to photographic negative *wax paper*, rendered sensitive by being saturated with a solution of the nitrate of silver and other chemicals. Another plan which has been proposed, as equally efficacious in putting an end to the system in question, is that of having a few words, or an ornamental design, struck off on the back of the genuine notes. These words or devices, by the process of sun-printing, are all transferred to the front of the imitation note, thus foiling the counterfeiters' art.

The paper on which the notes of the Bank of England are printed, is of the finest texture,—being strong it preserves its integrity, and as the bank never issues a bill a second time, they always present a new and clean appearance. Our banks issue their bills as long as they will hold together. The latter are easily torn and mutilated, causing a loss and destruction of no small amount to the public, and correspondingly great profits to the banks.

The reader will now provide himself with a well finished genuine Bank note, and also with a counterfeit, if one is at his command, and examine them minutely, as we go through with the description.

GENUINE BANK NOTE PAPER

Is always of a superior quality, possessing a fine, glossy surface, a substantial body, and in its *manufacture*, beauty and utility are successfully combined.

THE COUNTERFEIT

Is of a light, grayish color, soft to the touch, is generally fuzzy, is easily torn, and presents a finish very unlike the genuine.

ENGRAVING.

By the engraving is meant the lettering, scenery, and vignettes —commonly called pictures. A good bill is a pretty and perfect picture.

All Bank Note engraving, executed at the present day, is substantially alike. No difference can be discovered between any branch of it—whether engraved by one firm, or by another. The present system of bank note engraving, is acknowledged by brokers and others to be essentially perfect in every respect. A counterfeit has never yet been made which, on close examination, does not prove that the difference between a genuine and counterfeit bill is one, which if not always patent, is yet always eas-

2

ily discoverable. The Bank of England places no reliance upon any sort of engraving which may appear on the face of a bill. If we examine one of its notes, we will find that its denomination is expressed on the face of it in plain German text, to engrave which at the *most* costs probably not to exceed $50. The signatures are also all engraved. The eccentric ruling is executed on the plates by machinery, and the lines vary and diverge in so many ways, that after one set of plates are made and the tools destroyed, the bank itself cannot reproduce it or make a fac-simile of the plate. It proceeds on the principle that what one man can engrave, by hand, another can copy, but what one tool produces on a plate by eccentric ruling, operated on by machinery, no other tool can be made by the same machine to produce its exact fac-simile or counterfeit. Hence, bank notes *being* thus produced, and the tools destroyed with which the plates were engraved, the bank itself cannot produce others like them.

The whole face of a genuine bank note, under the present system of engraving, must be fine, even and steel-like, every object represented perfectly clear and distinct, with uniformity in workmanship, color, &c.

The banks of this country act on the principle that the more expressive and elaborate the engraving is made to appear on the face of the bill, the less danger there is of its being counterfeited.

COST OF BANK NOTES.

The cost of engraving some of the showy bills of our banks, with vignettes of Indians, faces of Bank Presidents, Franklins, Washingtons, Railroad Cars, Steamboats, Ships, &c., is in many cases from five hundred to one thousand dollars—all of which is done to prevent them from being readily counterfeited. The Bank of England, on the contrary, places no reliance whatever on fine and costly engravings. They print their notes with plates, the text of which might probably be executed for from forty to fifty dollars, and they have no counterfeits except those so clumsily executed as to deceive no one except the most ignorant.

The paper used on which the notes are printed, is, as we have before observed, of the finest quality, and constitutes no small item of expenditure in the "furniture" of a Bank. The engraved plates, the printing and the paper, cost in the aggregate our American Banks many thousands of dollars, this amount varying with the expensiveness of the engraving, and the extent of capital represented by the paper to be put in circulation.

GENUINE PLATES IN THE HANDS OF COUNTER-FEITERS.

Before proceeding to a detailed description of the several parts of a bill, it may be proper to allude to the manner in which Counterfeiters have been successful in getting possession of genuine plates.

There is a large number of genuine dies now in the hands of Counterfeiters which were obtained at a sheriff's sale of the property and effects of Messrs. Durand & Co., who formerly did an extensive business in Bank Note engraving. These dies were such as were then used by a number of Banks, and Counterfeiters by combining them in different ways, succeed in giving to *portions* of bills the appearance of genuine bills.

Banks now quite generally purchase and keep in their possession the dies of their bills ; in transporting the dies however from the engraver to the bank they have in several instances been stolen. With the genuine dies in his possession the Counterfeiter is of course enabled to produce a bill which will, so far as the *engraving* at least, readily deceive. Bank note engravers *may* fail, and even extraordinary diligence may not be sufficient to circumvent the thief, but it is believed that a careful attention to certain rules hereinafter given, with regard to the *general execution* not less than the engraved dies, will be sufficient in all ordinary cases of this nature to prevent imposition.

GEOMETRICAL LATHE WORK.

The Geometrical Lathe is a very perfect and costly machine, used by engravers for the purpose of producing very fine and beautiful circles or curvilinear figures. The work done by this machine may be seen principally on the counters and end pieces of bills.

GENUINE.

In a genuine bill, it will be found on a close examination of the lines or circles produced by this machine, that they seem to radiate from a *common centre*, and are *symmetrical* and *uniform*. The circles or counters on which the figures representing the denominations of the notes are placed, are made by this machine, and appear, on a close examination, beautifully interwoven and regular. In a genuine note, such is the extreme exactness of the work done by these machines, that there is never in the lines or circles, whether concentric, eccentric, or geometric, the slightest *possible irregularity or imperfection.*

COUNTERFEIT.

In a counterfeit bill, these lines and circles will be found, on close or even ordinary scrutiny, to be broken, blurred, and irregular. As, in counterfeits, the work is done by *hand*, instead of by machinery, the work is never perfect. In a genuine bill, as before observed, these circles on the face of the note seem interwoven, a network of circles, all perfect and seemingly starting from a *remote centre ;* in a counterfeit, they have the appearance of a mere *surface impression scratched* on the bill, and an observer, on scrutinizing the portion of the note made up of such circles and lines, can seldom fail to distinguish between the genuine and false.

PARALLEL RULING.

The Ruling Engine is used by engravers for the purpose of making the parallel rulings on notes, as also for shading letters, skies, and figures.

GENUINE.

In a genuine note, the characteristics of the lines made by this machine, in the hands of the engraver, are that the lines are of exactly the same *size*, are exactly *parallel*, and are at regular distances apart throughout ; they are fine, clear and distinct. The same criticism is applicable to the shading done by this machine, although, to a casual observer, it seems as if done with a brush ; when examined, it resolves itself into innumerable fine lines, each *perfect, regular* and *uniform*, and presenting a smooth and finished appearance.

COUNTERFEIT.

In stating the characteristics of the work done by this machine on a genuine bill, we may readily *divine* what is not and cannot be seen on a counterfeit. The delicate and perfect shading of the genuine engraving cannot be successfully imitated; the unevenness of the lines, and the coarseness and scratchy appearance of the counterfeit, done by hand, is easily noticed. It is but necessary to call attention to the work, and the difference is readily perceived—*breaks* in the continuity of the lines, deviations from parallelism, and variations in *thickness*, are the indicia of the counterfeit in these particulars.

MEDALLION RULING OR ENGRAVING.

Medallions are the raised patterns, or heads generally seen on bank bills. They are always copied from a medal or a raised pattern, and hence the name.

GENUINE.

The distinguishing characteristics of this work, as seen on a genuine bill, are, that in heads or figures, the perspective is perfect; the delicate shading caused by the approaching and receding of the lines, gives a *prominence* to the representation. If it is a head, the profile has all the boldness of a medallion on a medal. The *waving* of the lines is distinct, *perfect* and *continuous*, and the lines of which it is made up when crossing each other, do so in the centre, and form perfect squares. To give an accurate profile, requires elaborate care—such only as can be given by those who have made such work a life-study.

COUNTERFEIT.

The perfection to which line engraving has been brought in the representation of raised or Bas-relief figures, makes counterfeiting, in this particular, easily detected. In a counterfeit bill, the imperfections are seen in the *faulty* and *flattened* appearance of the figure. If a head is represented, or attempted to be, either an *unequal* and unnatural prominence will be given to one part, while another part is sunken, or a stiff, unnatural appearance is given to the figure. The lines, delicate, beautiful and complicated, in the genuine, which appear increasingly so when subjected to the more rigid scrutiny of the unaided eye, or whose beauties are more distinctly noticeable when examined through a microscope, in the counterfeit appear *increasingly* disfigured, imperfect, and scratchy, and the face, if the representation is a head, is expressionless ; cheeks are unnaturally prominent, or frequently graced with a spot in the centre as if caused by broken lines.

PERSPECTIVE.

GENUINE.

In a good bill, the perspective is perfect ; the delusion of a foreground and a background, giving to the representation the life-likeness of nature, is one of the most noticeable features of genuine engraving. The figures apparently the most remote, are as clearly and distinctly drawn as those in the foreground.

COUNTERFEIT.

In the counterfeit, unless the counterfeiter is an artist of the first order, which is seldom, if ever, the case, the perspective, or *vista-view*, is imperfect; the landscape is *flat*, the delicate tintings and shadings of nature are not copied; the sky is never distinct, and the clouds are always unnatural. The exactness of the work done by the Pantograph or Ruling Engine cannot be attained, much less copied by the graver in the hand of the artist unassisted by machines.

VIGNETTES.

By Vignettes is meant the ornamental figures or embellishments as pictures, seen on a bill.

The perfection to which the art of engraving has been brought, is nowhere more clearly seen than in the beauty and elaborate finish of these vignettes. We will pass in review some of the principal features of the more general figures and representations in use, and their more salient peculiarities.

PRINCIPAL FIGURES.

GENUINE.

In all bank bills, there is some particular figure to which prominence is given. In genuine bills, this figure will bear the closest scrutiny as to finish and symmetry—even to the minutest details.

COUNTERFEIT.

The principal figure on a counterfeit bill, may be equally prominent, but as it will probably be the best part of the engraving, it will serve by the glaring disproportion between it and its surroundings, as to labor and general appearance, only the more clearly to indicate its true character. The general criticism made as to a *blurred* and *scratchy* appearance of counterfeit bills, is *peculiarly applicable here.*

———————•◦•———————

PORTRAITS.

———

In no department of the counterfeiter's art, has he met with more signal failure, than in attempting to delineate the " human face divine ;" which as some one has beautifully and truthfully observed, "is the painted stage and natural robing-room of the soul."

GENUINE.

In the true bill, the mouth, eyes, and face, have an expression, clear and distinct. The hair, even in its most delicate wavings and strands, is accurately copied. The hands, and especially the fingers, will be found proportioned to the figure. The texture of the skin has not escaped attention, and indeed, in every respect, to the very minutiæ of detail, the portrait will bear close scrutiny. The more familiar portraits, as those of Washington, Franklin, Clay and Webster,—"the old familiar faces"—will strike the eye at once as being accurate, and the longer and more critically observed, the more perfect will the resemblance appear.

COUNTERFEIT.

In the counterfeit, the eye will be found not unfrequently without a *pupil ;* the delicate lines about the mouth omitted or constrained, so as to give a rigid and unnatural expression to that very important feature of the face ; black lines encircle the head, *spots* and broken lines appear on the cheek and neck,—none of which are seen on genuine bills. Bills may be so nearly worn out, it is true, as to make it no easy task to trace and follow out the symmetry and fineness of all parts of the portrait, but if any portion of the portrait is left entire, our remarks will be found applicable to that portion.

MALE AND FEMALE FIGURES.

GENUINE.

The general characteristics noticed above, under other heads, are applicable here. The larger proportion of vignettes will be found to consist, it is believed, of female figures. The drapery here is particularly noticeable. It will be found to represent beautifully the folds and texture of different kinds of cloth, and as it embraces the figure, will float and hang gracefully and naturally. Even the gloss of broadcloth, as in the garments of males, will be found transferred to the picture. In attention and fidelity to detail, a male or female figure, in a genuine bill, will have all the characteristics of the Pre-Raphaelite school of painting.

COUNTERFEIT.

We can add nothing here to what has been said before on other points in a bill, further than to call the attention of the reader to a scrutiny of the hands and fingers, the posture and proportion of the feet, the appearance of the drapery, the plaiting of the hair, and especially to the relative proportion of the different members of the body, and in a bad bill, in all these particulars, defects will be noticed as to *stiffness, indistinctness*, and an entire lack of finish in details, especially in those portions of the picture on which it may be supposed the eye will not readily rest.

FACES AND FIGURES IN DETAIL.

Before passing from the subject of Portraits, and male and female figures, it will, perhaps, be serviceable, though at the expense of a little repetition, to glance more particularly at the *details* of the figures. What we have said in the last two sub-divisions under those heads has reference to the "*tout ensemble*" of a bank bill, rather than to particular portions of it.

1. HAIR.—*Genuine.*—The *arrangement* is neat and easy. If curled, as in the case of female heads, the ringlets will be *graceful* and *natural;* on examination the *strands* will be discernable, and the difference between the straight black hair of the Indian, the close curled hair of the negro, the flowing locks of a girl, or the shaggy tufts of hair of a man, will distinctly appear. Look well to the texture of the hair. The reflection of the light upon it should be noticed.

   Counterfeit.—The arrangement of the hair is very often clumsy. The great difference between the hair as to texture and general appearance noticed above is not made apparent —it has a smoky, undefined and indistinct appearance.

2. EYES.—*Genuine.*—The eyes on a genuine bill are the most expressive feature, they give an individuality to the figure; the white of the eye is clear, as in a good painting, the eye

will watch, and seem almost to speak to you as you turn the picture from you.

Counterfeit.—More perfection has been attained by counterfeiters in representing the eye than any other feature of the human countenance. It is known that persons are generally apt to look first at the eyes of a picture, and hence the skill bestowed on this feature of the engraving. It is not exaggeration, however, to say that in more than half of the counterfeits the eye is a mere dot, of course expressionless, and that almost *invariably* the shading around the eye is too dark—frequently black—giving a frowning expression. The eye is frequently too far *recessed* into the head, owing to defects of SHADING—too *dark*, *black* and *heavy*.

3. CHEEKS.—*Genuine.*—The shading gives a full but natural prominence to the cheek; the high cheek bone of the Indian is noticeable; the wrinkles of age as well as the dimples and rounded lines of childhood, will appear, according to the age of the person represented.

Counterfeit.—Here the cheeks appear sunken; the individuality noticed above does not appear; the shading done by hand is always imperfect, and, if examined with particular reference to the prominence of the cheek, no one can be deceived.

4. MOUTH, NOSE.—*Genuine.*—The lines and shading about the mouth give it a prominence, owing to the lips, and the delicate lines at the end give it a natural expression; the dimples are rounded naturally—we may almost see the teeth—and in many instances the mouth will express something, and that, too, effectually. The nose, also, should and does stand out from the face; the shading of the lines at the base of the nose enables us as it were to see *into* the nostrils,

and from its base to the top the lines are so formed and shaded as to give it a natural—not too sharp or too flat—but a natural appearance.

Counterfeit.—The mouth on counterfeit bills is, almost without exception, bad ; it is either a *slit* on the lower part of the face having no expression, or else too deeply *indented* at the sides, giving it there a black unnatural appearance ; the curving of the lips is not seen, and character is wanting. The nose seems to be *laying on* the face instead of *standing out* from it ; there is no particular prominence given to the nostrils, and the shading necessary to give them distinctness is wanting. The *"isthmus"* between the nose and the *mouth* is not represented.

5. ARMS, HANDS, FEET.—*Genuine.*—Passing from the head we proceed to a critical notice of other parts. In a genuine bill the *arms* have given to them the curve and *plumpness* of nature ; the muscles in the brawny arm of the smith will be prominent ; the *articulations* of the elbow and wrist may be noticed ; the arm will be so shaded as to give it an appearance of roundness, that is, we can seem to see it as if a natural arm was resting *on* the paper. The same remarks are applicable to the hands and fingers—the joints and nails should be seen—the proportions of the hands to the body and of the fingers to the hand are just. The *position* of the hands is natural. If the hand is represented as upraised, the tension of the fibres and muscles will be seen. The *feet* are not so often noticed. But the same general characteristics will be noticed here as in the hands—the toes should be *defined*, and the shading should represent them separate and distinct.

Counterfeit.—We might say here summarily that the characteristics of the feet, arms and hands on counterfeits is their lack of symmetry; they are too flat; the rough lines of nature are *smoothed over;* the hands and fingers have no particular point; the fingers are not separated, or if they are, they are *jointless*, without proportion, and without life-likeness. The feet are seldom prominent; if bare, the toes are not *distinguishable*, the nails are not seen; if represented encased in boots or shoes, there will be noticed a lack of proportion; sometimes the heel is not seen on both boots. The remark we have had frequent occasion to make respecting the shading and bas-relief work may be repeated here.

6. DRAPERY.—*Genuine.*—To represent the drapery of a female figure requires careful and assiduous application. In the genuine bill the characteristics of the drapery are easiness, adjusting itself naturally and gracefully to the contour of the body. *Folds* of the cloth will be shaded so as to look *like* FOLDS. The *buttons* and button-holes on a coat will be perfect; and as in the case of a laborer, a *careless, easy* and yet perfectly natural appearance will be given to the vest and other garments.

Counterfeit.—The counterfeit bill is seldom if ever successful in any of these particulars. The dress, instead of appearing like cloth, or some cotton, linen or woolen substance, will look as if made of WIRE, *depending unnaturally* from the body, and in a very large number of cases which have passed under our observation, we have found the minor details of dress, such as buttons, button-holes, loops, fringes, &c., &c., entirely *wanting*. The counterfeiter is prepared for a *coup d'oeil,* but not for a rigid examination of his work.

We have now alluded to the most salient portions of engravings purporting to represent faces and other portions of human figures. Some other peculiarities we have not deemed it necessary to advert to in this connection, as well from the difficulty to distinguish in all points between counterfeit and genuine work, as also for the reason that the points above specially noted are *those which are the most noticeable*, and *afford the best evidence of the character of the bill.*

LANDSCAPES.

Landscapes, farm yard scenes, domestic animals in the foreground, railroad cars, ships and other representations of commerce, constitute, next to actual portraits or imaginary figures male or female, the larger proportion of vignettes seen on bank notes.

GENUINE.

In genuine bills *fidelity* to nature is closely adhered to. A perfect bill will constitute as pleasing a study as a painting by a master in landscapes, or the homelier representations of the *farm yard* or the *horse market*, as pictured by the brush of a Rosa Bonheur. New beauties will be revealed and repay the closest attention. Regarded either in its entirety or in detail, the picture will be found finished and accurate. The foliage of trees, the delicate shading required in the representation of clouds, are among the most difficult tasks committed to the engraver, but in genuine work, such is the exquisite perfection of the machines used, and the skill of the artists employed, that all the peculiarities of nature are copied. In cars and steamboats you will find the most delicate portions of the machinery represented—wheels, valves and boilers, screw-heads and bolts can be seen; smoke arises naturally from the engines and is clearly defined. In birds their feathers will be distinct and defined.

COUNTERFEIT.

A perfect landscape, one which will justify rigid or prolonged observation is never met with on the counterfeit bill. The landscapes look dark and forbidding, the trees appear as if blasted, and water and sky are undistinguishable. The lines in the ordinary figures, whether architectural or representing animals, are always poorly defined. Perspective so necessary to give realness to landscape in counterfeit bills is invariably *wanting*. Cars never seem to be in *motion*, and ships seem stationery rather than floating. The coarseness of the lines used to represent water effectually dispels the illusion of nature.

PRINTING.

GENUINE.

The most noteworthy feature of a genuine bill aside from the engraving is the artistic finish of the mere mechanical part of printing. The great care and attention with which all bank bills are printed, gives them a well-defined, legible, distinct appearance. All parts of the engraving will be found to have received their proper quantity of ink, and every portion of every figure will be found neatly and fully developed.

COUNTERFEIT.

It results from the secret manner in which the " black art" of the counterfeiter is carried on, the necessity to which he is subjected of doing by hand what machines do so much more perfectly for the engraver of genuine notes, that the printing of his *bill*, even supposing him successful in getting a tolerable engraving, is *poor*. The character of the printing is one of the most palpable badges of a counterfeit bill. The difference is so evident as hardly to escape attention when the observer's eye has been once directed to it.

LETTERING.

GENUINE.

The form and finish of the lettering on a genuine bill are among the first things to attract the eye. The letters and figures will be found *clean*, the lines perfectly *defined*, the curves and hair lines *delicately* and *exquisitely* executed. The round-hand writing on a bill, that is, the "Pay to Bearer," &c., &c., is black, equal in size, and smooth throughout.

COUNTERFEIT.

In counterfeits the lettering is poorly executed; a hazy *indistinctness* blends with the shading of the letters, the round-hand writing is pinched and stiff, the outlines never have the *sharpness* of the genuine, the curves will be found to be *broken*, as if executed by an unsteady hand.

INK.

GENUINE.

The characteristics of the black ink used by the engraver on genuine bills is, that it is of a *jet or glossy* black when first applied, and retains its original appearance for a long time. The red letters are composed of a network of red lines, and are frequently used for lettering and devices on the back of the bill. Different colors of ink have been experimented upon. Blue is used to some extent, also a pale green, but not generally, however. Engravers generally prepare their own ink.

COUNTERFEITS.

Partly owing to the printing, but attributable to a great extent to the ink used, counterfeit bills have a *dull* and *spiritless* appearance. The lines are indistinct, owing in a measure to the too quick absorption of the ink by the paper, and to its too easily *flowing*. The ink in a bad bill very soon fades and the entire face of the bill becomes thereby confused and indistinct. When a counterfeit bill is new, the defects of the engraving are most readily noticed; when old—perhaps a " premature old age" —the deadness of the vignette is one of the surest proofs of its worthlessness.

ENGRAVER'S IMPRINT.

On all genuine bills the engraver's name can be found in small, but distinct, neat and perfectly legible letters. Great reliance may be placed on the appearance of the imprint.

The counterfeit bill either omits it altogether, or in putting on the name of some responsible bank note engraving establishment, does it in a manner so bungling and defective that a person of ordinary intelligence can hardly be deceived. In one of the most successful counterfeits now in existence—twenties on the State Bank of Ohio—the engraver's *imprint* is not on a line, one name being much lower than the others. This is not uncommon in bad bills. A very successful counterfeit on the Chippewa Bank, in the word " York" in the imprint has a capital K. Similar defects in many other counterfeits might be referred to, but it is quite unnecessary, as the name of the establishment where the bills are engraved and printed appears on the bill, and thus acts as an advertisement ; it will be found to be one of the best executed parts on a genuine bill.

SIGNATURES.

GENUINE.

Any attempt to give an *infallible* test for determining the genuineness of a bill from the *character* of its signatures, would be of no practical utility. To persons accustomed to a particular signature, it may be a comparatively easy task to detect a forgery, not so, however, to others who are not experts. No reliance should be placed upon the handwriting alone. We may, however, state that there is a free, unconstrained and easy character to genuine signatures, in which respect they differ very often from the

COUNTERFEIT.

On the counterfeit note the penmanship is *generally* of an inferior character—not unfrequently the signatures of both Cashier and President appear to be in the same handwriting—and the " trail of the serpent" is seen in a *forced, cramped* and *unnatu-*

ral chirography. As cases are not uncommon of Bank Presidents and Cashiers, as well as Registers of bank bills, being deceived by imitations of their own signatures, it can hardly be expected that others may not be deceived also.

------◆◆◆------

RECAPITULATION.

We have thus given a series of rules which, if attentively studied, cannot fail to enable the reader to detect the frauds now so common in the issues of a coun erfeit paper currency.

A glance at the ordinary counterfeits will frequently suffice to convince a person who is acquainted with the requisites of a good engraving and the manner in which it is done, of these frauds. Others not so familiar, if the general appearance of the bill is not so glaringly base as to indicate at once its character, will need to pass in review the several parts, and scan critically the *frame-work* of the bill, the vignettes, the lettering, signatures and printing. If in any of these particulars the bill is deficient or imperfect, *reject it*.

We do not claim originality for these suggestions. They are the result not merely of our own experience and observation, but also of that of others whose business has brought them into daily contact with all kinds of paper currency, genuine and false; and while we do not claim infallibility for any *one* of the rules above given, taken separately, yet taken collectively they cannot fail to afford a sure clue to the detection of the false bill. It may be objected to the suggestions given in the foregoing pages that they assume the counterfeit engraver to be an ignorant or incapable man, unable to cope with his more honest compeers in the details of his profession. Such is comparatively true. Were the task of engraving committed to merely manual labor, unassisted by machines, the engravers of genuine and of counterfeit paper would stand side by side, and the chances for successful imitation and perfect engraving would be at least equal between them.

But on the side of the one are arrayed costly machines whose expensiveness alone presents a sufficient obstacle to their use by the counterfeiter, and this consideration of itself makes the contest between them unequal, so that it may be said with entire safety that it is impossible for an engraver of counterfeit bills to attain anything like the finish or perfection in his work which is everywhere seen in good bills. It is a source of regret, however, that in the bills issued by some of our Western banks, a niggardly policy of economy, *so called*, has obtained to so great an extent as to adopt, and use *inferior* rather than *first-class* engravings. This is true of a number, but not of all. A wise economy and a careful regard for the interests of the public demand at the hands of these corporations the very best engraved plates that can be obtained.

There are a few wood plates still used by some banks, which very soon become dull and spiritless, but they are fast passing into disuse, and the elegant steel engravings of the houses whose names were given in a former part of this Treatise, are taking their place. Another source of excellence in genuine bills which secures the highest perfection in the engraving, is, that in all the first class engraving establishments this business is divided up so as to make certain kinds of work a speciality with certain men, that is, no one man makes an *entire* vignette. One has devoted his attention exclusively to landscapes, another to domestic animals, another to portraits or fancy figures, and the *combined* talent, knowledge and skill of a number of artists is brought to bear on the production of an engraving which, when completed, may not be, and unfrequently is not, larger than a half dollar.

There are, however, a number of counterfeits in existence, in which portions of the vignette are genuine, and the remainder of the bill counterfeit. These counterfeits demand closer scrutiny than others, but it will be found on observation by the eye, and more especially by the aid of a microscope, that there is a gross inequality or disparity in the perfection or printing of different parts, and some small imperfections, as for instance in the engraver's imprint, or in a too *crowded* appearance of the figures for their surroundings, will betray their origin.

As has been before remarked in these pages, a perfect bill is a perfect picture, every feature, every department of the engraving will admit of a close and continued examination, and *lines*, not dots or *scratches*, will make up the lace-work, as it may properly be called, of the entire face of the vignette, as well as of the medallion and bas relief work.

ALTERED BILLS.

"The sublime mechanics of depravity" have been put into requisition in the execution of another species of fraud on paper currency, that is, in altering the denominations of bills from a smaller to a greater number, or in altering the name of the bank as to its locality.

To accomplish this alteration of a bill as to its denomination, counterfeit counters are printed in the place of the genuine one, or are pasted over them. When so altered, if the bill is held up to the light, the change will be readily noticed; the paper there will be found thinner, more uneven, and the bill will present as to these parts a ragged appearance. If the back of the bill is examined, the *pasting* and patching is easily detected by a change of color and thickness of paper. The pasted *edges* may easily be detected in this way. If the title of the bank, or its locality, is changed, which is done not unfrequently, where one of two banks in different States bearing the same name, fails, and the name of the *State* in the broken bank bills, is changed; this alteration may be detected in the same manner. Around the alteration the paper will be found blurred, and dimmed, and torn. Hold it up to the light—look at the back of the bill.

The acid used to eat out the original lettering or counter, stains the paper and the ink blends with it, giving an indistinct appearance to that portion of the bill.

PHOTOGRAPHED BILLS.

Photographed bills present new difficulties. The ease with which bills have been copied by this process, is attributable, doubtless, more to the ink which has been used than to anything else. The chief characteristic of a photographed bill is the appearance of the paper. It always looks *greasy* and *transparent*—*feels* like oiled paper. The impression seems to be on *both sides* of the bill, and is very *indistinct*, and particularly towards the ends of the bill, the *centre* of the bill being generally much darker than any other portion of it.

To make a perfect photographed copy, requires more skill than counterfeiters generally employ, and the number of counterfeits produced in this manner is not as yet sufficiently great to demand special attention. Old bills, it is believed, are photographed less easily than new issues. Bills having lettering or devices on the back, cannot be copied by this process, and it is hoped that the use of a different kind of paper or ink than is now in general use, will prevent all successes in this department of deception hereafter. Blue colored paper when photographed is of a white color. The following recipe for detecting photographic counterfeits has been used to a considerable extent, and is believed an infallible test:—Take a lump of cyanide of potassium, wet it, and apply it to the surface of the impression. If it be a photographic bill it will immediately turn white, the potassium dissolving out the nitrate of silver, leaving the blank paper; while if genuine, it will remain unchanged.

MONEY AND LIFE.

———————

"Young man, qualify yourself for business. The professions are full; and the age demands it. Educate yourself for business. A business man for the farm, the counting room, and commercial pursuits, and you will succeed now and hereafter."—CLAY.

In closing this work, devoted as have been its pages to the most mercenary of all subjects, Money, it may not be regarded as inappropriate to add a few homely suggestions as to the relations of Money to success in Life.

To those who duly estimate its importance, and the stern solemnity of the duties it imposes, Life can never be regarded as a mere speculative venture, a game of hazard, governed by no principles of action, acknowledging fealty to no maxims of movement. Such a theory of Life is essentially false, and the young man who starts out upon its perilous voyage, relying only on fickle Fortune—chartless and compassless—can hardly fail to meet with disaster and shipwreck, as the rewards of his imprudence. No, the battle of Life is to be fought with the coolness and courage of science, its fortresses are to be taken, not by storm, but by resolute, determined and discreet movements. It is a siege —not a guerrilla skirmish.

MONEY GETTING.

There is a class of transcendental teachers, who affect contempt for money, who, with an air of pompous superiority, speak of it as gross, and its pursuit as grovelling and incompatible with the "dignity of human nature." It is unnecessary to waste words on these visionary notions. It is sufficient for our present purpose that success in business life, as popularly understood, is the amassing of a competency—the getting of money.

"The smell of all cash is good," says Vespasian, and much as we may affect to despise money or wealth, as an incentive to business pursuits, yet our daily injunction when interpreted by "our daily walk and conversation," sounds wonderfully like that given in some one of the plays of "rare Ben Jonson,"

"Get money, still get money, boy,
No matter by what means."

This may be bad philosophy, and still worse morality, but if put to the rack or the confessional, would not the larger proportion of us be obliged to admit, in all honesty, that if not *ours*, it is at least the life-motto of our neighbors—emblazoned on *their* escutcheons, and displayed in golden capitals on *their* phylacteries. Some one has said that, "The gold eagle, the silver dollar, and the copper cent, is the American trinity," but, rightly considered, the getting of money, so far from being an ignoble pursuit, should commend itself to every honest mind. The odium has attached less to the *result*, than to the *mode* of getting money. The "pleasures of poverty" is a theme, on which poets may dilate, but in the refrain of *their* song, the hearts of very few of us ever join.

SUCCESS IN BUSINESS.

We are so constituted, physically and mentally, as a *nation*, that there is to us all an irresistible charm in business. Were it otherwise, it would be difficult to frame a hypothesis which would satisfactorily account for the large and daily influx into commercial circles of those whose youth, talents, and prospects, entitle them to be regarded as the "flower of our country." But of this large number, hopeful, earnest, "eager for the fray," how very few ever attain the goal of their wishes, or acquire that competency which, when they started out in life, seemed like the grapes which tortured the vision of Tantalus, so near that the hand could almost reach them, but when sought to be brought within the grasp, eluded the touch or were scattered to the winds!

Could a "table of mortality" be prepared, which would show the ratio of successful to unsuccessful merchants, it would be found that Dame Fortune has been exceedingly chary of her favors. Misfortune and adversity would seem to have ever been in the ascendant. But we hazard nothing in saying, that of the number of wrecks in business life, much the larger proportion may justly be said to have been entirely *unnecessary*, that is, that they might have been avoided had not these unfortunates been ignorant in very many instances of the fundamental canons of business. It is not to be presumed that any rules or hints can be given in these particulars which will be infallible, or which will *demonstrate* a man into a fortune, as the demonstration *follows* from the axiom in Euclid, but the suggestions which are here given, are given only as beacons to illumine the pathway over which all must pass—as *adjuncts*, not *substitutes*.

BUSINESS EDUCATION.

"Let no man enter into business while he is ignorant of regulating accounts; never let him imagine that any degree of natural ability will supply the deficiency or preserve multiplicity of affairs from inextricable confusion."—JOHNSON.

We place a practical education as first in the order of requisites to success. The age of nursery tales has almost gone by. The generation of remarkable men, who, without *any* education, have achieved success, has almost passed out of memory. More than ever before is the necessity now urgent, that the young athletæ, "in the strife for gain," should be skilled, at least theoretically, in the *principles* of that conflict in which he is about to engage. He must be educated, if at all, with a strict and especial reference to business pursuits, if he intends to become a business man. A perfect acquaintance with "the tale of Troy divine," will afford a person very little assistance in understanding "the laws of trade." The mysteries of Eleusis differ essentially from the mysteries of the counting room or those of the bank director's office.

The calculation of Parabolas and Ellipses will not solve " daily balances," and " profit and loss " require for their proper appreciation something more than an acquaintance with Greek syntax. There is such a thing as a business education, as distinguished from the education doled out in modern colleges. An education which shall acquaint the farmer with the properties, qualities and varieties of his soil and woodlands ; which shall teach the artisan the theory of his art, and open up to the aspirant for mercantile honors, all the ways and byways which he must explore in order to reach his goal.

The young man intending to devote himself to the profession of law, has his " moot court " in which are epitomized the forms which he will have to use, and the struggles which he will be obliged to undergo in his future professional career. Should not the young man, designing to follow the business of a merchant, have also his *moot counting room*, in which he may see the mode of keeping books, and the details of active and actual business, and have expounded to him his rights and liabilities, as a member of the business community ? Should not his school-room be an epitome of that larger school-room, the busy, bustling world, in which he is soon to enter ?

With such an education, and such an one *is* attainable, the young man is already equipped for duty and action. The transition from the school-room to the desk, the work bench, or the farm, is easy, gradual and natural. Unlike his confrère who may have sought similar instructions in so called " classical seminaries," and at the expiration of his four years study, rolls off from the lap of his " *Alma Mater*," a useless and impracticable thing, *he* is versed at once in the *modus operandi* of his business, and from *his* superior education for actual business life, is the better fitted to cope with his fellows, profit by their prudence and avoid their errors.

ADVERTISING.

The Press is a powerful auxiliary to the business man. The experience of every successful merchant, proves the profitableness of advertising. Advertising has been reduced to a system with men in many different kinds of business, and the result is seen in the success which has, almost without exception, attended it. It is true that "people think in herds," and it is also true that in the formation of *their* opinions, the Public Press is entitled to the priority. We advise any young man, as the first step to be taken by him, to *advertise*—using the Press, however, as an auxiliary with the same good sense and judgment which are needed in every other department of business. The secret of successful advertising is sometimes said to consist in saying enough to *excite* without *satisfying* curiosity. This, however, is but a half truth, and has reference more to the *sensation* advertisements of semi-humbugs than to the kind to be used by ingenuous business men. The object being admitted to be to attract *attention* to the *wares* and not to the *seller*, that system of advertising is infinitely to be preferred which keeps the merchant behind rather than in front of his counters. We look to the advertising columns of our journals for very unromantic announcements, and the intellectual gymnastics of a business clown floundering through printers' ink may cause a smile but seldom do they produce conviction. While the rates of advertising here are considerably less than in England, " the fast shored isle" is able to present many more instances of advertising on a large and profitable scale than is seen here. The victories in this field have been won by *persistent*, *repeated* and *generous* publication, and although no one can predict that success *will* certainly follow, it is sufficient to know that *success has* always been achieved by those who have made the Press the right arm of their power.

It has been often observed that the merchants, in every city or village, who most frequently bring their goods before the public through this medium, are the best patronized. It evinces life and energy of character, and we may in this connection, with safety, paraphrase Pope's maxim as one borne out by universal mercantile experience, that,

"Whate'er is best advertised, is best."

BUSINESS MANNERS.

No department of Ethics is deserving of more careful and assiduous regard than that which pertains to the etiquette of business life. The annals of mercantile experience furnish a few instances of men who have achieved success in disregard of all those social and business amenities which no where shine more brightly than when seen in the counting-room or the work shop. But these are exceptional cases. Mental idiosyncrasies and moral delinquencies may be measurably overlooked in him who relies upon the public for his support, but boorishness of manners, incivilities and grossness, never. Gruff, insolent and bearish Dr. Johnsons may be tracked and followed by toadying Boswells, but no such fawning attentions are ever shown the merchant or the artisan by any of their customers. Suavity of address and civility of manners can be appreciated by all, and, more frequently than other qualifications give to the individual his reputation and character as a man of business. These are the most salient points in the business character, and for that reason need stricter attention.

OPPOSITION.

Opposition is an element in a successful career deserving attention. Kites rise against and not with the wind. Opposition strengthens individual reliance, sharpens one's wits, and is a constant whip and spur to lethargy and indolence.

Competition and strong and unrelenting opposition, in developing the best faculties of our nature, have made more fortunes than tame quiescence ever did. Hardship is the natural soil of manhood and self-reliance. When a man in starting a business is violently opposed, and especially if the opposition comes from those engaged in a business similar to his own, rest assured that it is because of his superior merit or the superior quality of his wares. Such competition strengthens him and his business. A well-regulated commerce, says Addison, is not like law, physic or divinity, to be over-stocked with hands, but, on the contrary, flourishes by multitudes, and gives employment to all its professors.

Cunning men not unfrequently resort to an expedient which indicates their acquaintance with the value of opposition. They improvise a sham fight between themselves and some other person, and thus by *seeming* to be persecuted, gain the honors as well as the *emoluments* of martyrdom.

If the humbug-monger can resort to this artifice to increase his business, no good reason can be suggested why opposition, however violent or bitter it may be, or competition, however brisk or active *it* may be, should not be turned to the advantage of the party or person against whom they are specially directed. Men do not thrive by inaction, and no business can be said to be founded on a sure and permanent basis which does not grow strong by the assaults made upon it, or acquire thereby

> " A towering and deep-rooted strength of soul
> " Which like the oak might shake in summer winds,
> " But stript by winter, stands immovable."

AVOID CREDIT.

"Mr. Speaker," said a distinguished but eccentric American Statesman, "I have found the philosopher's stone, it is "Pay as you go."

The policy of American business men, for the last 20 years, if the late crisis affords any clue to it, seems to be expressed in Butler's lines, to

> " Run in debt by disputation,
> " And pay with ratiocination."

The credit system which seems to some extent to be a necessary evil, has expanded to a magnitude overwhelming, and disastrous in its consequences to all branches of commerce and trade.

The lesson of the late monetary pressure whose chilly and paralizing touch is yet felt on the body politic, is a warning againt expanded credits.

Credit, like borrowing, "dulls the edge of husbandry." Were we to write over the doors of nine-tenths of the mercantile houses which have failed during the past two years, the cause of their demise, or if not already dead, of their suspended animation, it would all be comprehended in the two fatal monosyllables "charge it."

It cannot be expected in the present organization of society and of business customs, that credit can be at once entirely abolished, but that it can with entire safety be greatly lessened, admits of no question. The cash system when systematically pursued, produces more *true* friends to the merchant as well as the mechanic than any other, it dispenses with more than half the machinery of the counting room, and like charity, " is doubly blessed, it blesses him who gives and him who takes."

Hard times generally begin in one's own account books, and the gaunt spectre of Bankruptcy is ever hovering near those time yellowed entries of " old accounts" and " slow notes."

MERCANTILE HONOR.

"The best laid schemes of mice and men gang aft a-gley." It is not always possible for the merchant to accumulate a fortune, but it is always possible for him to maintain his integrity, to keep his escutcheon untarnished by a resort to the petty tricks and devices which ever indicate baseness. If there is any spectacle which commends human nature, it is that of a man whose honor has not suffered by contact with his wares. Such men there are, and though at the end of their career it may not be possible for them to point to large fortunes as the result of their business career, the possession of a reputation to be transmitted to their children, of uniform honesty and unblemished honor, still entitles them to be regarded as having conquered a success greater even than that of the millionaire.

The "Tricks of Trade," of which so much is frequently said in connection with business pursuits, whatever may be their apparent advantage, impair confidence, and in the end injure those who practise them more than those upon whom they are practised.

BUSINESS LIFE.

Were the same reflection and consideration bestowed by the aspirant for mercantile success before entering upon his particular vocation, which are generally given to other pursuits, the number of shattered hopes and wrecked lives would be infinitely less than is now witnessed. It is a common error, that any one can succeed by any means soever he may choose to adopt in the ordinary departments of trade, and as a consequence we see daily exemplified before us the spectacle of men engaged in business for which they have no particular adaptation, nor tact, nor talent, and who go to their counting-rooms and work-benches daily,

"———— as a galley slave,
Scourged to his dungeon,"

whose whole business career is but a succession of blunders, and

4

whose life is but a burlesque on Human Nature. Nor, until business men shall be inspired with the dignity of their calling, until they shall cease to look upon trade as a mere art in which the premium is awarded to trickery and low cunning, until they shall regard it as a noble science, a system of comprehensive and ennobling principles, and enter upon it with the same chivalrous and generous devotion which leads the Divine and the Jurist to adopt and pursue callings less in the avenues of trade than theirs, can it be expected to be otherwise. And especially to the American merchant is it important that he should feel impressed with his responsibility, not merely to his immediate neighbors, but also to that imposing Guild of which he is a component part.

The counting-room, the workshop, and the farm, have each battles as stern as any ever achieved on the fields of Agincourt or Crecy, and as worthy of renown and remembrance as the loftiest successes ever achieved at the forum or on the " hustings."

We have not alluded to the ordinary virtues such as economy, temperance, application and integrity, as elements in a successful business career, for such we conceive to be axioms which do not admit of discussion or question. We have assumed the business man who may read these suggestions to be actuated in his desire for success by laudable motives, and to be above the use of chicanery and fraud to compass his ends. To such we commend these homely suggestions, and in parting with our reader we can assure him that it is as true of individuals as the philosophic Heeren observes of nations, that " A NATION IS NEVER DESERTED BY DESTINY SO LONG AS IT DOES NOT DESERT ITSELF."